Seducing the Sitter

An Erotic Taboo Babysitter MFF Threesome Romance

By

Emma Jade

Seducing The Sitter
An Erotic Taboo Babysitter
MFF Threesome Romance

Copyright © 2019 Emma Jade

There were a few things that Madison expected when it came to her job. When she was asked to babysit, she expected that there would be problem children or those that got a little too nosy; asked questions a little too direct. She expected to come across 'adult' items every now and then, but this really was the last thing Madison would have ever expected to find while she was at work.

The two children she was looking after were already asleep. They'd gone up to bed at least an hour ago by now, leaving the young woman to settle herself in and relax until their parents returned home.

Of course, it wasn't the best work she could be doing. Most twenty-two-year-olds had a full-time job or were in school, but Madison was just doing what she could to make ends meet by doing something that she actually enjoyed doing.

Bored, she'd decided to curl up on the couch with a soda, and put on a movie. The system they had for storing them was a little strange, though Madison was far from complaining when they seemed to have hundreds of movies stored as video files on a thumb drive stuck in the side of the television.

She knew there was a slight risk that the films had likely been downloaded, as some of them had some rather weird titles, or the file names seemed to just be dates and times. It was difficult to filter through them and figure out what was what, since the files themselves didn't seem to have any actual thumbnails - just black space where an image from the movie would usually be.

It was really weird, and put a strange feeling in the pit of Madison's gut, though she pressed on, selecting a random file and playing it on the television. Immediately sound started blaring and made the young woman nearly jump out of her own skin, quickly lowering the volume so that it wouldn't wake the children upstairs.

She'd forgotten just how loudly they liked to play their own movies. Once Madison had finally calmed down a bit, she seemed to finally process just what she was looking at. It seemed like... The bedroom of the couple she was babysitting for. And was that...?

"Mm... Come on, Michael. I know you can do better than that," Carrie hums, a moan slipping out of her as she slowly rolls her hips on top of her husband, keeping her hands braced on his chest to keep her balance. He lets out a choked groan, his head falling back into the pillows as he practically arches under her, trying to plant his feet on the bed to buck up into his wife's body himself.

She doesn't seem to be having any of it, though. Carrie leans back a bit and grips one of his thighs, pushing it back down to the bed. The action only presses the woman's chest out more, and Madison can't help the way that her eyes follow the line of the woman's body, her mouth watered slightly at the sight.

"Please... Fuck, Maddy," Michael groans out the words, and Madison swears her heart jumps into her throat, her eyes widening a little at what she just heard. There's no way he had actually moaned her name, was there? Why would he moan her name? Maybe she'd misheard it -

"Come on. Don't you want to fuck my tight pussy?" Carrie breathes, and Madison can see the shudder that runs through Michael, nodding his head quickly and trying to buck his hips up into his wife, his actions almost desperate.

"Yes - God, Fuck yes. I want to bend you over and pound your sweet little cunt, Madison," The words sent a tingling pleasure coursing through what felt like her very veins themselves, the crotch of her panties feeling soaked already.

There was no way that she was hearing this correctly. No way that the couple really sought after her in such a way, or even considered having sex with her like this. Was this honestly what Michael thought of her every time he'd seen her?

She had to admit - She was kind of impressed by just how much control Carrie had over her husband, and if she was honest, the woman had control over her at the same time. She could feel her breath caught in her throat just watching and hearing the two of them. The sounds alone would have been enough to rile her up, but the fact that they were talking as though she were there?

Heat was pooling in the pit of her stomach at the thought that they wanted her like that. They were a well-established couple, with what seemed to her like an amazing sex life. What could a twenty-two-year-old like her provide that they couldn't get themselves?

Madison couldn't tear her eyes away from the video no matter how hard she tried, shivering a little herself as she watched them. She could feel herself getting more and more turned on the longer she watched. It was getting impossible to ignore the feeling of wetness forming between her legs, her gaze frozen on the television in front of her.

Slowly, oh so slowly, her hand slipped from where it had been resting on her thigh to press over the front of her shorts, slowly rubbing at herself. It felt wrong to be doing this to something so personal and private, though they had included her, in a way, even if it wasn't the most conventional.

Madison never would have guessed that either of them had seen her sexually like this before. But she had plenty of evidence right here - in the form of the couple fucking while pretending that the wife was her.

"Ah, Fuck! Come on, Michael. I know you want to fuck her harder than this!" Carrie's voice was practically in her mind at this point, her moans settled comfortably in her senses. Just the thought - The thought of Michael fucking her while Carrie watched…

She'd never had any interest in that sort of thing before - in being watched like that, but clearly, her body was interested, judging by how wet she was, how her clit felt like it was throbbing at the thought of the older man's cock spreading her open and filling her up so full... Maybe he'd even cum inside of her, and Carrie would probably make him eat it right back out of her.

Madison couldn't help the sharp gasp that left her lips at that thought, slipping her hand into her panties and letting out a shaky little moan as her fingers found her clit, slowly rubbing loose circles around the sensitive skin. It sent little sparks of pleasure racing along her spine, trembling and spreading her legs the slightest bit as she relaxed back into the couch.

This was easily one of the most "out there" things Madison had done. She'd only had a few boyfriends in the past, so although she'd had sex before, there had never really been a chance to explore what she liked or disliked. At least anything she had tried had been on her own, and a lot of things sounded better in theory.

She couldn't tear her eyes away from the video playing low on the television, swallowing thickly at the slight glow on their skin from the thin sheen of sweat. Madison's eyes followed a bead of the liquid as it's coursed its way down between Carrie's breasts and over her stomach until it was lost in the neatly trimmed curls of the woman's pussy, the clear shine of her own release showing on her folds, as well as her inner thighs.

It made the young woman's mouth water at the idea of tasting her juices, and apparently, in the video, Michael was having the same thought. He made a faint noise in the back of his throat, hands moving down to grip at Carrie's thighs and giving her a pleading look, his tongue pressing across his lips. She seemed to decide to humor him for now, moving to straddle higher up his body, until she was hovering just over his face.

"I've wanted to get a taste of you for so long, Maddy," Michael groaned, drawing his wife closer and burying his face between the plush of her thighs, kissing along them before he finally set to work dragging his tongue over the soaked lips of her pussy, kissing and sucking eagerly at her core.

Finally, the video paused, only for it to rewind about ten seconds, just before Michael had spoken. To hear her own name said like that, and imagining the older man's tongue flicking over her clit like that, dragging over and fucking into her pussy... It drove her absolutely mad.

Her fingers almost exactly followed the path of Michael's tongue, tracing over her own slick folds and circling slowly around her clitoris. She had to press her hand over her mouth to try and keep herself from waking the boys she was babysitting with her noises.

On screen, Carrie's moans were only getting more and more desperate, her hand curled tight in her husband's hair and all but riding his face. And for what it was worth, the man was taking it like a champ, and looked more than happy to do so. He was still rock hard, precum spilling from the slit and dribbling down the side of his erection, a small pool of the liquid gathering on his stomach.

A louder, more guttural moan tore Madison from her fantasies of licking Michael's cock clean, as her gaze instead focused again on Carrie's twitching thighs, the pace of her hips getting more erratic as her climax approached.

Honestly, Madison couldn't say that she was much further behind. Her own hips were bucking into her own touch as she fingered herself, two fingers pressed into her pussy as she ground the heel of her palm lightly against her clit. She was soaking wet, and even with her panties slightly pulled away from her body, she could feel then soaked through down far enough to reach her ass, her juices flowing almost freely over her asshole itself.

It was impossible for her to hold in her own little whimpers and moans, going so far as to bite down on the flesh of her free hand as her own orgasm hit her like a brick wall, a choked noise tearing from her throat. Her pussy practically convulsed tightly around her fingers, spilling even more of her fluids into her likely ruined underwear.

Her thighs twitched and trembled with the aftershocks of it as she slowly came down from the high of her climax, knowing that as soon as she was able to get her legs working well enough to stand up again, she would need to run to the bathroom and most likely ditch her panties entirely. There was no way she could comfortably wear the undergarments as they were anymore.

Holy shit, if just the thought of having sex with the older couple made her cum like that, she could only imagine what it would be like to actually do it.

Now that gave her an idea…

Things went smoothly for the rest of the evening. As soon as she could, Madison went to the bathroom to slip out of her underwear, tucking it into her shorts pocket for now, considering there weren't many other options in the way of places where she could hide her dirty underwear.

Carrie and Michael soon returned home, and despite the fact that they were fully dressed, Madison couldn't shake the mental image of Carrie's bare body or their words from her mind.

Just being near them made her excited, in a way that she was a little embarrassed to admit. She was in the kitchen when they came home, announcing themselves when they came in the front door. Michael was the first one she saw, stepping into the kitchen and offering her a warm smile.

"Hey, Maddy. Did the boys go down easily?" He asked, walking towards the fridge. He had to step past her, lightly touching her waist almost as a warning as he passed behind her. The young woman couldn't help the shudder that ran through her at the brush of his hand, her mind immediately thinking back to the video she had seen earlier.

"Huh? No, Yeah. They were perfect," She replied easily, fighting the urge to press back into his touch, or reach out to hold his hand in place, rather than letting it be a simple fleeting touch. Hadn't he said something in that video about how he fantasized about bending her over the counter?

"That's good," Carrie hummed, stepping into the kitchen herself and settling into one of the chairs at the island. Almost wordlessly, Michael opened the fridge and got out a water bottle for her, taking the lid off before he set it in front of her. She simply gave him a little nod, before her gaze was more focused on Madison.

"They like you, you know. The boys. Every time we mention getting a babysitter they nearly beg for us to call you," The older woman's gaze was heavy, and Madison could have sworn she could feel exactly where her eyes were looking, even when she seemed to drop her gaze below Madison's face.

"I'm glad they like me," she spoke up after a moment, fidgeting a little and tugging down the hem of her shirt, as much as she'd rather tug her shorts down and lean over the countertop. She did do the latter part, however, leaning over the marble top of the island, trying not to think too hard about the lower cut of her shirt.

She could feel their eyes on her, though, and part of that was intoxicating. How had she never noticed it before? Both halves of the couple seemed to not be able to take their eyes off of her.

"Do you need a ride home tonight? I wouldn't mind dropping you off," Michael spoke up after a few moments of silence, seeming to force his eyes away from her and back towards his wife. She gave him a knowing look, taking a slow sip of her water before she pushed herself away from the island.

"Of course not! It's already dark out. Way too late to walk home safely," Carrie spoke up immediately, her hand coming to rest at the small of Madison's back. It was something that she had done in the past, though before the touch had felt almost motherly. It was far from that now, the entire air around her taking on another tone entirely.

Carrie's touch felt teasing now, and Madison could feel goosebumps rising across the skin of her arms. She swallowed around the lump in her throat, slowly pulling away from the touch and straightening up.

"I'd really appreciate that," she spoke up herself after a moment, rubbing at her arm to try and settle the bumps on her arms, caught between hoping that her reaction was seen, and also entirely missed. As much as she loved the thought of... being a part of what she had seen, her nerves were also affecting her as well.

"Let's get going then," Michael nodded, stepping out of the kitchen and grabbing the keys from the table in the hallway. "I wouldn't want to get you home too late," He pulled his jacket over his shoulders, waiting for Madison to go and grab her bag before they both step outside into the night, heading for the family's car.

Madison carefully slipped into the passenger seat, buckling her seatbelt and settling in for the drive home. Between the sense of awkwardness that seemed to come from Michael, and her own thoughts plaguing her mind, there really wasn't much in the way of conversation. They both stayed quiet until Michael pulled into the parking area of Madison's apartment building, offering her a warm smile.

"Have a good night, Maddy," He finally spoke up once he had put the car in park, reaching over the center console to gently rest his hand on her thigh. His touch was warm, and it made Madison shiver lightly, heat pooling in the pit of her stomach as her eyes drifted from his hand back towards his face, wordless for a long moment.

"I... Yeah, you too," She finally managed to choke out, her face heating up at the arousal growing in the pit of her stomach. She could feel herself getting wet again at all of the thoughts running through her head, embarrassed and panicking a bit at the realization that her juices weren't going to do much other than wet the crotch of her shorts, and that would be far too difficult to try and hide from Michael's sight.

"We were thinking of going out again in another couple of days. Do you think you'll be free Friday night?" He asked her suddenly, reclaiming his hand and settling back into his seat to watch her curiously. Madison felt like her mind was reeling, trying to process and focus on what was being said to her.

"Friday?" She asked, watching him nod, and still not fully processing the movement, "I'm free Friday. Don't have anything planned, at least. If you text me the details, I'm sure I can be there whenever you need me," Madison pushed herself up out of the car, biting at her lower lip.

"Yeah, of course," He hummed, the grin on his face entirely missed by the younger woman as she hugs her back to her chest, quickly offering a smile and a "Thanks for the ride" over her shoulder. It isn't long before she's shutting the door and hurrying to the building's door, trying to ignore the feeling of her own juices starting to slowly drip down her inner thighs.

Madison can hear the car pulling away as she slips into her building, heading upstairs to her apartment. Her heart didn't stop pounding until she had closed and locked the door behind herself, and even then her pulse was still racing, her breath coming a little faster than usual from her walk up the stairs.

She slowly relaxed again, her breathing slowing down to normal until she was able to push herself away from the door, toeing her shoes off and shuffling them towards the stand with the rest of her shoes. Madison then stepped further into her apartment, dropping her bag onto the couch and heading into her bedroom.

Madison was more than ready to crawl into bed and simply fall asleep, but she knew that she would need to shower and get herself cleaned up, both from the day itself and from her earlier activities. It didn't help that she was still slightly wet from all of the excitement of the day.

The young woman sighed, pulling her shirt off over her head and tossing it into the dirty laundry as she passed through her bedroom, her bra coming off next. Madison was quick to undress and toss her clothes into the laundry basket, forgetting that she had put her panties in the pockets of her shirts earlier, and entirely missing the fact that the lace undergarment was now missing entirely.

With the water turned on, and steam soon rising to fog up the bathroom mirror, Madison climbed into the shower and began to clean herself off, washing her hair and running her fingers through the long strands with a content sigh. The warmth of the water helped to ease the slight ache in her muscles, and it temporarily brought her mind away from her own arousal and the wet feeling of her own juices dripping down her inner thighs.

It was hard to tell which liquid was which; when she was entirely dripping with water. It didn't take long for Madison to get herself cleaned up and ready to get out, though... with the calm of the shower overtaking her system, her mind couldn't help but return to the arousal that had come up just from being in the car alone with Michael.

She was really going to have to get her hormones under control if she was going to be babysitting for the couple again on Friday, though right now it was really hard to resist the urges that made her fingers itch, her mind wandering to one of the few toys she kept in her nightstand. She wasn't entirely exhausted yet, and surely an orgasm would help her sleep better - they usually did.

With that plan set in her mind, Madison turned the water off and stepped out of the shower, grabbing one of her soft, plush towels and drying herself off with it. Wrapping the material around her body, the young woman made her way back into her bedroom and bent over to dig one of her toys out from its hiding place, tossing it onto her bed and stepping away once again to finish drying off. She pulled a tank top on but decided not to bother with panties or her usual sleep shorts.

Instead, Madison crawled into bed, settling onto her back and slowly spreading her legs. Even with her shower washing away the evidence of her arousal, she was still certain that she'd be able to take her toy without the assistance of lube, her hands wandering lightly over her collarbone. One hand stayed at her chest, fingertips slowly rubbing over one of her nipples and twisting it lightly.

It was far too easy to imagine her own touch as that of Carrie, the mother's tongue expertly pressing and licking over her nipple as her hands wandered elsewhere. It was hard to keep her own touch slow and languid, highly doubting that the woman would be so eager to make her immediately cum.

It was torture in all the best ways, to touch herself like this. To move slowly, imagining that it wasn't her own touch. Usually, she would just rush through this is an attempt to get herself off so that she could sleep, but at the slower pace… it was driving her crazy, her clit already close to throbbing in a plea for attention.

Her free hand skated down over her stomach, soon pressing down between the lips of her pussy to seek out her clit, already wet and warm there. The initial touch had her biting back a small gasp, fingers slowly teasing around the sensitive skin with a feather light touch.

It really was almost too much for her to handle, desperately craving the toy inside of her, and the rush of an orgasm, though she knew that if she rushed if - or when she was in bed with Michael and Carrie, it would most likely disappoint them. She had to be good. Had to hold off a little longer, until she could feel Michael's thick cock pushing into her, most likely forcing her open beyond anything she'd ever gotten from her previous boyfriends.

Just the thought of it alone was enough to have her gasping out, reaching for the dildo she had grabbed from her bedside table. She quickly popped open the lid of the lube, spreading a bit over the toy before pressing it between her legs, the dildo easily sliding into her wet pussy. She bit at her lower lip to try and keep in her own sounds.

Though she never had any proof of it, she had always been nervous that her neighbors could hear her when she did masturbate like this and had always tried to be quieter just in case. She kept up the same habit even now, the only sounds in the room consisting of her own soft whimpers, and the wet noises of the toy plunging into her wet pussy over and over and over again.

It was both heaven and hell, tormenting herself like this. She fucked herself hard and fast with the toy, though her own straying touches were softer and almost feather-light, both sensations complete opposites of each other, but building into something much bigger. Something so much more intense than she had ever felt before.

It felt entirely impossible to even begin to hold her noises in anymore, gasping and letting out desperate sobs of pleasure every time the toy struck deep inside of her, her eyes rolling back in her head slightly as her back arched off of the bed, warmth spreading through every nerve ending in her body.

It was getting to be too much. It was all so much - the filthy sound of the toy fucking into her, and the overwhelming feelings of pleasure were threatening to break her. It really only took a few moments longer for her pleasure to build to its climax, squirming and pressing her face firmly into her pillow to try and muffle the loud, guttural moan that tore its way out of her chest, the fluids of her release leaking out around the toy and dripping down the crease of her thighs, staining the sheets underneath her with her own moisture.

Madison could do nothing for a few long moments other than go limp on pliant on her bed, her chest heaving with each breath she desperately sucked in as the waves of her orgasm slowly washed away, her fingers still twitching with it for a good couple of minutes before she was finally able to lift her head.

She couldn't really do much, though, barely able to pull the toy out of herself and toss it back to the nightstand where it had come from before she simply rolled over on her bed, not even bothering to pull the covers over her body before she passed out, falling into a deep sleep.

*

The days passed quickly, and before she knew it, she was waking up on Friday morning to a text from Carrie, making sure she was still alright to watch their children that evening. She was told that they were going out to dinner and would be out most of the evening, so she was expecting it to be another quiet night where she was able to put the two boys to bed and spend the rest of the evening to herself relaxing.

It was one of the better ways to make the money she needed to make rent, and with the added bonus of getting to see Carrie and Michael dressed in their best at the end of the night, it was something she had absolutely no desire to turn down.

Madison had been running errands all day, stopping by the bank to deposit some cash from her last babysitting job. She ended up going to get groceries as well, taking them to her apartment to put them all away.

It wasn't until about 5:00 pm that she began to get ready to head over for her babysitting gig. It really didn't take her all that long, brushing out her hair before she pulled it into a ponytail, sighing and straightening out the fabric of her skirt.

After gathering a few things to help her prepare for the night, she slung her bag across her body and grabbed her keys before she headed out for the evening, making sure to lock the door to her apartment before taking off.

It didn't take long for her to make it to Carrie and Michael's home, walking up to the front door easily and knocking at the dark wood. She took outside for a few long moments, expecting that one of the boys would answer the door to let her in, or that Michael would.

Instead, Carrie soon opened the door, standing there in what seemed to be her normal day clothes. Assuming that she simply hadn't gotten ready yet, Madison offered her a warm smile, making her way inside when the older woman stepped back and invited her in.

Everything seemed entirely normal, other than… the noises. The house was almost deadly silent, clearly no sign of the two boys that she usually babysat, considering that they were loud and rambunctious, and had a habit of running to greet her at the door.

"Where are the boys?" Madison asked, her eyebrows furrowed in confusion as she looked over towards Carrie, clearly not understanding what was happening.

"Come sit down, Madison. I think we all need to talk," Carrie said simply, gesturing into the kitchen, where they had chatted a bit just days ago before Michael had taken her home.

"Did… I do something wrong?" The younger woman questioned, anxiety spiking in her system as she moved to sit at one of the bar stools lined up on the far side of the island, her hands shaking slightly. Had Carrie found out that she had watched one of their 'home movies'? Maybe she knew that Madison had masturbated to it, and was going to fire her!

"No, No. You didn't do anything wrong, dear," Carrie hummed almost immediately, leaning against the opposite side of the island and watching Madison's face almost with amusement, "Michael told me that he found something of yours after he dropped you off."

Madison only grew more confused. She hadn't forgotten anything, had she? She'd had her phone last night, and nothing had been missing from her bag… What could she possibly have forgotten?

It wasn't until Carrie raised her hand that she understood exactly what it was that she was talking about. Hanging from her fingers was the pair of panties that Madison hadn't realized she'd been missing, her face burning bright red at the sight of them.

"I - I didn't know those had fallen out of - I can explain," She finally managed to choke out, her hands shaking slightly. She really was going to lose this job, wasn't she? They were going to be disgusted by her.

"There's no need to explain, really. If anything Michael was the one confused," Carried hummed, stepping around the island. She dropped the panties onto the countertop, sliding onto the barstool next to Madison and leaning in a little closer to her, "He almost thought you were trying to seduce him," She let out a little laugh, reaching out to rest her hand on Madison's shoulder.

"Are you going to fire me?" The younger woman asked, tensing up a little and letting out a shaky breath. Carrie just laughed again, shaking her head.

"Fire you? No, of course not. The boys adore you. You're their favorite babysitter. We just wanted to see if you might be interested in… a sort of bonus, for all of your work."

"A bonus?" Madison tilted her head a little, raising an eyebrow. She shivered slightly as Carrie's hand moved down along her arm, before resting on her thigh, fingertips just under the hem of the skirt she had worn today.

"Yes. You see… It isn't just the younger boys that have a bit of a soft spot for you. Michael has grown rather attached to you as well, as I'm sure you saw last time you were here," The older woman slowly rose from her seat, gesturing for Madison to follow after her.

She really couldn't have disobeyed if she wanted to, Carrie's presence was intoxicating, and Madison was admittedly more than a little interested in just what sort of thing the older woman meant. Last time she was here? Oh - That video. She swallowed thickly, biting at her lower lip.

"I really didn't mean to watch that video, I swear. I had thought that you simply downloaded your movies and had them saved like that. I've been to homes before where the parents did that to avoid spending a fortune on movies for their children," Madison tried to explain quickly, not quite processing that Carrie was leading her through an empty home, up to the couple's bedroom.

"Madison, you aren't in trouble for anything," Carrie quickly assured her, a knowing smirk tugging at her lips, "In fact. We were going to see if you were interested in joining us sometime. Considering you've already seen that video, I'm assuming you've realized that Michael is… attracted to you."

Madison paused, blood rushing to her face and warmth dropping into her stomach like a lead weight. "You… You want me to fuck your husband?" She managed to squeak out after a moment. It was hard to deny that she had been thinking about it all week, but to hear it offered out to her…

To see Michael through the open crack of their door, wearing nothing but his boxers, the front of them tented in obvious arousal… It was something else entirely. Something that made her both soaking wet and shaking with nerves all at the same time.

"That's exactly it, dear. I want you to let my husband and I fuck you. I never said that I didn't want a little action," she hummed, looking over her shoulder towards Madison, "If that's what you want, of course. We're not about to force you into anything. But you should know… the boys aren't home at all.

We sent them out to stay with another babysitter until I go and pick them up tonight. So if you'd like to do this, now would be the perfect time."

Madison blinked in surprise at the older woman, unable to do much more than watch as she stepped closer before a finger was pushing her chin up, and her eyes were forced to meet those of the woman she'd been babysitting for.

"How does that sound to you, Madison? Would you like to join us for the evening, or would you rather I take you back home and we forget it was ever mentioned?" Carrie asked, lightly stroking her thumb over the plush of Madison's cheek.

She felt as though she'd been rendered speechless, swallowing around a lump in her throat and spending a moment simply opening and closing her mouth, trying to decide exactly what to say. Isn't this exactly what she had been wanting all week? Had been craving their hands on her - fucking herself every night to the thought of Michael's cock in her, or even to the thought of Carrie herself fucking her into the mattress.

She takes a moment to breathe, her throat suddenly inexplicably dry, before finally speaking up.

"I... I want that," she admitted, licking her lips and feeling her gaze drift again to that open crack in the doorway, where Michael now was sitting up, looking more alert and almost... excited. Could he hear their entire conversation? Did he know exactly what he was getting, now?

"Good," Carrie hummed, smiling warmly at her and pushing the door to their bedroom open. She took Madison's hand into her own, leading her inside and making sure she closed the door behind them, even if no one else was in their home.

"Hi, Maddy," Michael breathed from where he sat on the bed, most definitely knowing exactly where this night was going now... The younger woman offered him a shy smile, shifting her weight a little.

"Michael," she answered lightly in greeting, her fingers fidgeting slightly with the hem of her skirt. His gaze seemed to fixate on that, eager to see her body without all of the layers covering her smooth skin.

"You should take these off, pet," Carrie whispered, stepping up behind Madison. Her hands ghosted lightly over Madison's shoulders before moving to the front of her blouse, the older woman's chin resting on her shoulder as she slowly undid each button on her blouse, exposing more and more unmarked skin for Michaels eyes to devour.

Madison shivered under all of the attention - under the intensity of their gazes on her. This was far from anything that she was used to, and as she was further undressed, it only made her feel more embarrassed, though at the same time it was... almost empowering to her, to see the looks in their eyes. To see just how badly they wanted her. And while it wasn't quite as obvious with Carrie, Michael's arousal was right there, more than noticeable considering that he was just wearing boxers.

It made her mouth water, and by the time her blouse was off and her bra was undone, she was craving the weight of his cock on her tongue. She couldn't help but swallow thickly at the thought, and Carrie seemed to somehow know exactly where her mind was at, looking over towards Michael and speaking with the same soft-yet-commanding voice that she'd been using on Madison.

"Take those off, Michael," She said simply, gesturing towards his boxers. The older man seemed more than eager to get the material off, quickly pushing them down his hips and tossing them to the laundry basket in the corner. He laid back once he was undressed, his arousal resting heavy against his stomach, precum already starting to bead at the tip.

Whatever Madison had joined clearly must have started before she'd gotten there, considering just how flushed the man was, and how hard he was. It almost looked painful, how deep of a color the head of his cock was.

"You want to taste, don't you?" Carrie's voice returned to the space next to Madison's ear, and a tingling tremble shot down her spine. She quickly nodded, a low sound building in the back of her throat, close to a whimper.

"Yes ma'am," Madison breathed, polite as always, even in such a situation. She could feel Carrie's smile against her skin, one of the older woman's hands guiding her bra off of her, before the hand slid down the smooth plane of her stomach, dipping down into the waistband of her skirt and panties.

The noise that came out of Madison then was louder, a moan being drawn from her as skilled fingers circled her clit, lightly rubbing over her using the moisture that had gathered between her legs. Madison could only feel herself get more turned on by the action, leaning back against Carrie slightly and letting out a shuddering breath as she was touched.

"Michael. Come," Carrie demanded, her free hand pulling Madison's skirt up to bunch around her waist, before pulling the material of her panties aside. It completely exposed her soaking wet pussy, making the younger girl flush and try to hide her face from the embarrassment, though she couldn't help but peek between her fingers as Michael obeyed.

He moved across the bed, before getting off of it entirely and got to his knees on the floor. He looked more than eager for what he knew was coming, even if Madison herself had no clue.

"Spread her legs a little wider… Please," Michael spoke up, adding the last word almost as a forgotten afterthought. He leaned closer to their bodies, helping to coak Madison's legs apart, and drinking in the sight of her bare pussy, reaching out to idly trace his fingers up along the trail of her juices that had dripped down her thigh, before rubbing over the lips of her pussy, spreading her open so that he could better see her.

There was only a moment before his mouth was pressed against her, tongue eagerly dragging over her hole to taste her, before pushing into it slightly every so often. It was immediately close to too much, making Madison gasp out and try to press her thighs closed. However between Carrie's hands holding her legs open, and Michael's face pressed between them, it was nearly impossible.

She couldn't do much but tremble and let out desperate, gasping little moans as Michael ate her out, almost as though this had been his first meal in weeks. He was clearly trying to please her to the best of his abilities, and with all of the frustration she'd been feeling this week, and how worked up she'd gotten just from Carrie's hands on her, there was no way that she was going to be able to last very long at all.

The older man's tongue eagerly lapped up every drop of the juices spilling from her pussy, working over her clit and dragging his tongue between her folds. It was driving her absolutely wild, her chest heaving under Carrie's attentions as she hit her climax, a gush of fluids coating the lower half of Michael's face and streaming into his waiting mouth.

He seemed more than happy to have been made a mess, though, a low groan leaving him as he practically drank up Madison's release, slowly dragging his tongue over her to clean her up just a bit.

It wasn't until Madison looked down that she realized he'd been touching himself through this whole process, a surprised little whine slipping from her throat at the thought. It was clearly enough to amuse Carrie behind her, the woman chuckling low in her ear before pulling away entirely, and padding over to their large bed.

She undressed as she walked, slowly revealing the dark lace of lingerie that had been hidden underneath her lounge clothes, sweatpants slipping down her hips to show off black material that hugged her curves like a second skin, making Madison's mouth water at the sight.

"Come on. You two. You aren't getting all of the pleasure," Carrie shot a grin and a wink over her shoulder, crawling onto the bed and settling back against the headboard, her legs falling apart easily. It was easy to see how wet she already was as well, and Madison found herself moving forward before even Michael could.

She moved up the bed, leaning down to press reverent kisses along the older woman's inner thighs, slowly tracing her lips up along her legs until the simple scent of Carrie's body overpowered any of her other senses. It sent a shudder through his senses, almost dazed as she mouthed over Carrie's pussy through the thin material of her underwear, dragging her tongue over the space where she knew the other woman's clit was.

It was addicting - Absolutely intoxicating to be tasting another woman like this. It was something that Madison had never once imagined herself doing, yet here she was, moving aside Carrie's panties and pressing her mouth and tongue to the other woman's cunt like a man starving for food he hadn't tasted in years.

It was an entirely new experience, and Madison was more than happy to continue, even with the press of Carrie's hand curling into her hair, holding the younger woman close to her body with a pleased little sigh. It only added another layer to it all, knowing that she was pleasing the other woman, that her own actions were enough to encourage the juices that were dripping down Carrie's inner legs.

Madison was so caught up in what she was doing that she almost completely tuned Michael out, jolting in surprise when she felt his hands on her hips, fingers rubbing over her pussy before two of the thick digits pressed into her. It made her gasp out against Carrie's skin, her hips wiggling back into the attention slightly.

Michael spent a good minute fingering her open, adding to the intensity of it all. His fingers dragged over her inner walls in a way that made her clench around them, body already craving more - craving something bigger filling her. Something that the older man seemed more than eager to provide her with, his fingers leaving her body almost as suddenly as they had pressed into her.

Something warmer and thicker soon took their place, rubbing against her dripping pussy before pushing into her, slow and steady. It had her pausing in the movements against Carrie's body, face turning to press against the woman's thigh as she was spread open and stuffed full.

It was enough to have her trembling and gasping softly for breath, already feeling on the edge once again. Madison felt so wonderfully full, a feeling that she knew she would come to crave, and would easily begged for if she had to.

And then he began to actually move, and it lit every one of her nerves on fire, pleasure blazing through her system and burning her up from the inside out.

"That's it. You've been waiting for a chance at that pretty pussy for so long, haven't you?" Carried spoke up suddenly, the sultry tone in her voice dripping down Madison's spine. It made her whimper, body clenching slightly around Michael's cock. She already knew. She knew how badly he'd been wanting her. Saw how desperately he had fucked Carrie in that video, imagining that it was her. And now he had her, wrapped snugly around his cock.

He nearly gasped out a "Yes", only confirming what Madison already knew, as he gripped onto her hips and began to really fuck into her then, slamming his hips forward against her. The action pushed her back against the moist skin of Carrie's pussy, the younger woman letting out a loud moan before the noise was muffled.

It was clear what they both wanted, especially with the grip returning to Madison's hair, both holding the strands out of her face and pushing her in closer.

She could feel every other thought leaving her, Madison's mind only thinking of one thing as the couple used her warm, pliant body for their own pleasure.

More.

She slowly got back into the rhythm of their actions, her tongue eagerly lapping over Carrie's pussy again, before she focused on the other woman's clit, tracing absentminded shapes over the sensitive skin and doing her absolute best to please the dominating woman.

It was more than intoxicating, more than just pleasure alone. It felt right. And all she wanted was more. She wanted to be like this so much more, wanted to make Carrie feel good, wanted to feel the throb of Michaels cock in her soaked pussy over and over again.

It quickly reached a peak that Madison could hardly even comprehend. All she knew was that one moment she was gasping between licks to Carrie's clit, the next her face was nearly forced impossibly further against the woman's body, and a sharp taste coated her tongue, making her let out a surprised moan. Warmth spilled into her only a few short moments later, a soothing heat that settled deep in her stomach.

Michael slowly pulled out of her with a shaky groan, and that warmth leaked out of her, adding to the mess dripping down her thighs and leaving a slight puddle on the sheets underneath her. A clear mark of what had occured soaking into the material beneath them.

Madison felt dazed, finally allowed to pull away from Carrie's body. The lower part of her face felt wet, as did her thighs, though she could hardly even think about that at the moment, sitting up on the bed and giving a dazed little laugh.

She knew she looked fucked out, and she had no doubt her skin was flushed, rising and falling with her heavy breaths as she tried to regain the bit of air she'd lost while nearly drowning in Carrie's pussy.

Michael was still behind her, settling on the bed himself and gently rubbing his hand over the side of her thigh, almost as though he were trying to soothe her. It felt nice, the warm heat of his large hand. She offered him a little smile before her gaze fixed itself back on Carrie, the other woman watching them with an amused little hum.

"Did you two enjoy yourselves?" She asked, chuckling softly and sitting up herself. She reached out and lightly touched Madison's thigh as well, her own hand resting over Michael's. Madison nodded in response, making Carrie's smile grow a little warmer.

"Good, Maybe we can convince you to come back for another round some time, then," Michael whispered behind Madison, his lips lightly pressing to the skin just under her ear.

Yeah… She liked the sound of that.

Follow *Emma Jade*...

Get notified when new books are released!
Visit bit.ly/emma-jade-newsletter

Check out other exciting stories written by *Emma Jade*... visit amazon.com/author/emmajade

- **Submission to My Billionaire Boss**
  After Nadia moves to a new city in an attempt to get away from an abusive ex, she finds herself a job as the executive assistant for billionaire Josh Sutton. With his help, she's able to finally get rid of her ex – but she soon learns Josh is after much more than that...

  Josh is looking for a special kind of relationship, one that leaves Nadia feeling unsure, but aroused. When she bites the bullet and agrees, it begins a long and exciting journey with a wide variety of steamy situations.

  From million-dollar yachts and mansions all the way to a trip to Paris, Nadia's wild adventures are just getting started...

- **The MILF Housewife Next Door**
  Brooke is a confident, sexy housewife in her mid-forties. In an open-marriage with her wonderful husband Brayden, she gets to enjoy a multitude of sexual escapades.

  Brayden hires Matt, a shy and inexperienced young man who lives next door, to trim the hedges. What starts out as a simple chore, quickly transforms into a much "dirtier" job.

  Join us for this sizzling, salacious tale of MILF debauchery. This is one mom that you'd really like to fornicate.

- **From Tragedy to Trio: An Erotic Threesome Romance**

  Logan is numb, the world spins before him as he listens to his prognosis from the doctor. He has cancer and he's going to die.

  Brian and Chanel, Logan's two best friends, lives are rocked when they find out. Struggling to cope with it, they vow to help Logan to deal with the pain, no matter how tough it might be.

  What starts out as a situation that appears to be dire, results in one that will rock their world.

  What happens to Logan? Will Brian and Chanel be able to weather the storm of losing their best friend?

  Read this heartwarming tale of love, sex and raw emotion to find out!

- **Caught in the Flames: A Life Saved, An Erotic Group Romance Kindled**

  Finding her unconscious, trapped at the center of a warehouse fire, these heroic firemen saved her life.

  Aubrey feels compelled to reward her heroes with an experience that they will never forget.

  Join us on this titillating adventure where Aubrey becomes the center of the gang in this hot MMMF tag-team visit to her microbrewery. Believe me, this is one messy party that you're not going to want to miss out on!

- **Indecent Grades: An Erotic Student / Professor Taboo Romance**

  Erika is about to fail a class that she desperately needs to pass in order to obtain admission into college.

  Professor Charles Quinn, a strict no-nonsense professor, won't bend the rules for any student, no matter how smart, beautiful or kind they are... that is, unless...

  Erika is desperate and she'll do whatever it takes.

Can Erika gain a passing grade? Will she get to go to college? Can she break the professor's strict, no second-chances policy? Nobody has ever been able to before, but she has no choice, she's got to try.

Envelop yourself in this exciting taboo student/professor erotica tale to find out...

- ## My Memoir Into Submission
  Amelia meets her neighbor, Josh, a friendly good looking man who turns out to have some secrets. These secrets lead Amelia from a life of mundane routine to one of excitement and fun; while sexually empowering her through her discovery of what she really needs, and who she really is - a submissive.

- ## The Vixen Voyeur: A MFF Menage Romance
  What starts out as an innocent cycling ride, ends up in a voyeuristic adventure for Brian, a recently divorced gentleman who is struggling from an onset of loneliness.

  What becomes the object of his desire, quickly becomes a catalyst into a life he could never have imagined...

  Join us on this sizzling tale, where not one, but two sexy little vixens make Brian's dreams come true!

- ## The Panty Snatcher: A Femdom Panty Fetish Romance
  David has always had a panty fetish. His pent-up lust for panties controls his impulses. This time, it gets him in trouble...

  "He had just made up his mind to follow his instincts without shifting his yearning eyes from the fashionable unmentionables."

  Lisa, David's next door neighbor, catches him red-handed stealing a pair from her laundry. Not only is she going to teach him a lesson, she's going to have fun with it.

  "Firstly, from now on, you'll address me as Goddess. Secondly, I want you to strip for me."'

Delve in and enjoy this female domination tale and explore the world of panty sniffing, facesitting, underwear fetish, foot fetish and more.

- ## Dirty Work: An Erotic Construction Site Romance

  Sarah is a dedicated, hard-working foreman at a construction company. She is called upon when nobody else can solve issues at construction sites, traveling the country to fix messes that others have caused. Her dedication to her work and lack of time for any semblance of a relationship has caused her to be incredibly lonely.

  Grant is a construction worker, an uneducated street kid turned construction worker who never knew anything else. He is straightforward, honest and hard-working. His friendliness and charisma enable him to rally his team to success.

  Sarah and Grant could not have been more different, but difference has no voice when it comes to sex and love.

  Delve into this erotic tale of fantasy turned reality. Get ready, you're about to get your hands dirty...

- ## A Night Turned Threesome

  A 30th birthday celebration turns into a 'dirty 30" one when an old school friend shows up and turns into a tantalizing twelve hour threesome

- ## The Secret Cuckold

  Nathan becomes a cuckold, but his wife doesn't even know it. Having his wife cuckold him, gets him off in ways he couldn't even imagine.

About *Emma Jade...*

Emma started writing stories when she was seven years old. She wrote essays, articles, and over two million words of nonfiction before turning to fiction in 2013.

She watched erotic romance authors having way too much fun, and after writing her first erotic romance, she was hooked.

She writes erotic romances based on her real-life experience primarily featuring swinging, BDSM and cuckolding.

Emma lives near Toronto and likes reading, travel, and heavenly hash ice cream.

Made in the USA
Las Vegas, NV
23 March 2022

46176523R00023